THIS CANDLEWICK BOOK BELONGS TO:

_____

_____

_____

For Holly, Karen, Ann, Karina, and Yvetta

First paperback edition 2013

The Library of Congress has cataloged the hardcover edition as follows:

Menchin, Scott.
Taking a bath with the dog and other things that make me happy / Scott Menchin. — 1st ed.
p.   cm.
Summary: In order to answer her mother's question about what would make her smile,
a girl first asks various people, animals, and even the moon what makes them happy.
ISBN 978-0-7636-2919-9 (hardcover)
[1. Happiness—Fiction. 2. Questions and Answers—Fiction.]   I. Title.
PZ7.M522 Tak 2007
[E]—dc22   2006046288

ISBN 978-0-7636-6335-3 (paperback)

13 14 15 16 17 18 SCP 10 9 8 7 6 5 4 3 2 1

Printed in Humen, Dongguan, China

This book was typeset in Alghera.
The illustrations were done in ink and watercolor,
with digitally colorized backgrounds.

Candlewick Press
99 Dover Street
Somerville, Massachusetts 02144

visit us at www.candlewick.com

Taking a Bath with the Dog

and Other Things that Make Me Happy

SCOTT MENCHIN

CANDLEWICK PRESS

I miss
your smile
today,
Sweet Pea.
What would
make you
happy?

I don't know.

What
makes
you
happy?

Taking a bath!

What makes you happy?

Counting.

What makes you happy?

What makes you happy?

Shoes.

What makes you happy?

Playing with my hair.

What makes you happy?

Digging.

What
makes
you
happy?

Stripes.

What makes you happy?

Sleeping
upside down.

What makes you happy?

Smiling.

Hmmmm . . .

Yes!

I'm happy when I . . .

Tickle my baby brother. Jump rope.

 Bake cookies with faces.  Ride my bike.

Chew peas one at a time.  Make a wish.

 Stay up late.  Paint on eggs.

Make faces.  Hold my breath underwater.

 Stick finger puppets on my toes.  Sing.

Slurp spaghetti.  Look at my reflection.

 Dance with my shadow.  Play dress-up.

Sit in my dad's chair.  Blow bubbles.

 Drink tea with Grandma.  Play drums.

Pretend I'm a monster.  Swim at night.

 Lick sprinkles off ice cream. And . . .

I'm happy
when
I'm taking
a bath
with
the dog!

Mom, you're smiling.
You must be happy too!

Scott Menchin, the author-illustrator of *What if Everything Had Legs?* and the illustrator of several picture books, including *Song of Middle C* by Alison McGhee, has this to say: "I wrote this book after years of looking for happiness. What I eventually realized was that different things make different people happy—but what made me happy was doing what I enjoyed most. That might be simple things, like listening to a favorite song or watching my daughter eat breakfast. The real trick, I learned, was to make a list at the end of each day of all the good things that had happened. And when all else fails, even just putting on a smile can make you happy. It's a medical fact!" Scott Menchin lives in New York City with his wife and daughter.